For Nel-erella! – M.S.

To my dear uncle,
my best fan – B.B.

First published in 2016
by Scholastic Children's Books
Euston House, 24 Eversholt Street,
London NW1 1DB
a division of Scholastic Ltd
www.scholastic.co.uk
London · New York · Toronto · Sydney · Auckland
Mexico City · New Delhi · Hong Kong

Text copyright © 2016 Mark Sperring
Illustrations copyright © 2016 Barbara Bongini

ISBN 978 1407 16248 5

10 9 8 7 6 5 4 3 2 1

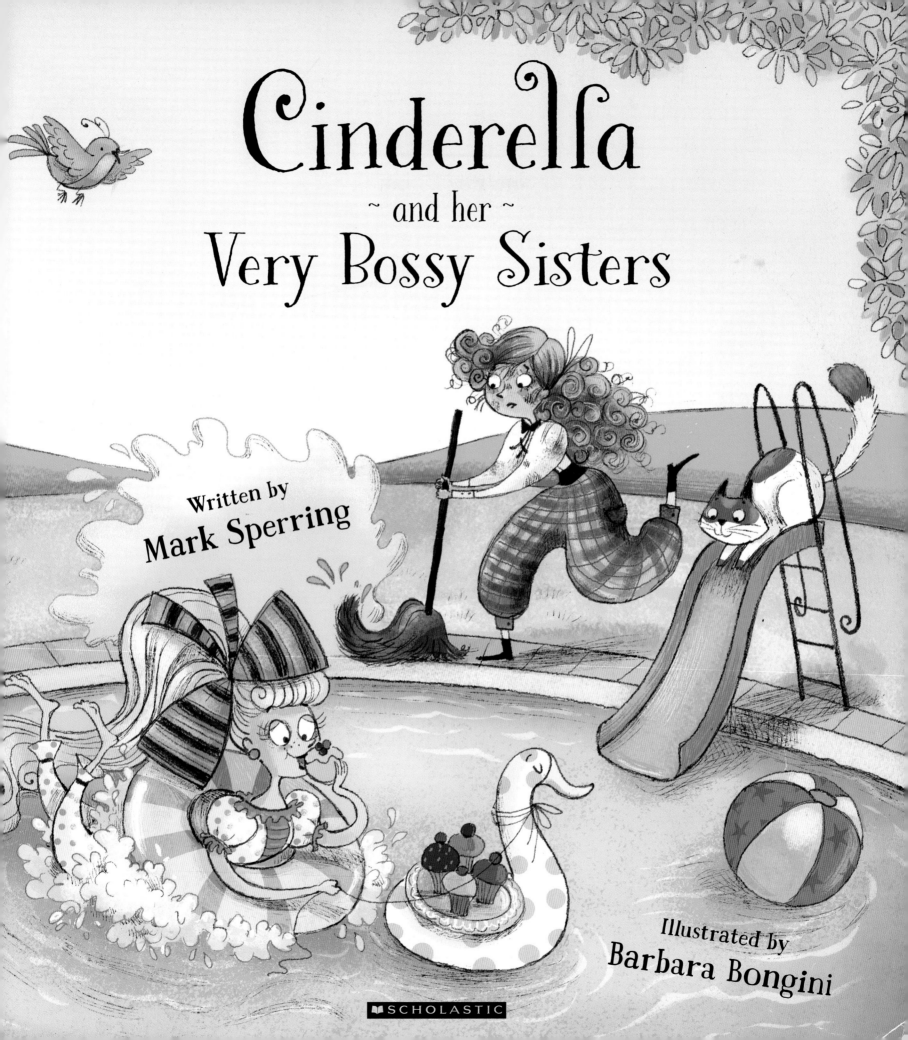

Once upon a time there lived a girl called Cinderella.
If she wasn't COOKING, she was CLEANING.

If she wasn't FETCHING, she was CARRYING.

And if she wasn't doing any of those, she was busy…

...doing something else entirely!

Now, if you're wondering why Cinderella was always so busy, it was thanks to her two sisters, Gerta and Greta, who NEVER stopped bossing her about...

Cinderella, fix that lamp... (It might have blown a fuse.)

Cinderella, take a hammer – build a shelf for all our shoes.

VAGUE

One evening, when Cinderella was busy repairing a clock,
re-heeling a shoe and repainting the WHOLE kitchen,
an invitation dropped through the door.

"It's from the Palace," gasped Cinderella.
"We've all been invited to a ball... TONIGHT!"

"Well," said her sisters, "YOU can't go, you've nothing to wear,
but at least you can help US get ready..."

"Cinderella, run our baths,
Cinderella, fix our hair."

"Find our great BIG spotted bloomers
(we threw them down somewhere...)"

"Fetch our dresses from the wardrobe
and our shoes from off the shelf."

"Tighten up our corsets—
we can't do that ourselves!"

"Squeeze the pimples on our chins,
pluck that hair out from our noses,"

"Drench us both in perfume,
till we smell... SWEET AS ROSES!"

"There, there..." said a voice, as Cinderella watched her sisters leave,
"everything will work out TICKETY-BOO, you'll see!"
And there, to Cinderella's surprise, stood an ACTUAL fairy!

"I'm your Fairy Godmother," said the fairy with a friendly
wave of her wand. "Now, would you be an absolute PEACH
and fetch me a PUMPKIN, thanks ever-so!"

Moments later, Cinderella's Fairy Godmother was hard at work. First she waved her wand over Cinderella's scruffy old clothes... And **look** what they became!

Next, she turned the pumpkin
into a **beautiful** carriage,
complete with four white horses.

The final MAGICAL touch was a pair of glass slippers...
As soon as Cinderella slipped them on, everything – her dress,
the coach and all the stars in the glittering sky seemed to be...

...coated in fairy dust.

"Now, be sure to be back by the last stroke of midnight," warned Cinderella's Fairy Godmother.

"That's when my WONDERFUL spell will come undone."

When Cinderella turned up at the palace **everyone** wondered who she was...

Perhaps it's Princess Pomp-Pee-Domp of Pop-Dovia?

OR Lady Loopy-Droops from Loch-Livia.

For NOBODY recognised Cinderella in all her finery.

As for the Prince, well... he was **totally smitten.**

"I was hoping you'd dance with me all night and right the way through till morning!" he spluttered...

Then, of course, they DID dance... But not for as long as either would have liked...

For, at the first stroke of midnight, Cinderella remembered her fairy godmother's warning and, before everything could turn back into old clothes and pumpkin mush, she fled...

"Come back," cried the Prince, "I don't even know your name!" But Cinderella was already gone and all that she left was a single glass slipper that had fallen from her foot...

The next day, Cinderella's sisters were in a TERRIBLE mood.

It's not **fair!** they moaned.

The Prince didn't even **dance** with us!

And they might have spent the whole morning sulking
if there hadn't been a knock at the door...

It was the Prince!

The Prince pointed to the glass slipper and explained he'd been searching all morning, in EVERY house, for the young lady whose foot fitted the shoe.

"You see, I HAVE to find her," he blushed, "so we can both live HAPPILY EVER AFTER."

Cinderella's sisters tried the shoe on first...

"It's a PERFECT fit," said Greta painfully. "The VERY shoe I wore last night!" cringed Gerta. "All we need is a little extra help..."

Cinderella, bend our toes back, Pull the shoe over our heels.

Cinderella, crumple up our feet, Ignore our painful squeals.

Cinderella, push your hardest
Till that shoe fits like a glove.

Ow! Ow! Ow! Ow! Ow! Ow! Ow! Ow! Ow! Ow! Ow! Ow!

Cinderella, almost... nearly...
Just give it one last shove!

"Sisters..." sighed Cinderella,
after much yelping and screaming,
"perhaps *I* should try the shoe."

And LOOK...

...it fitted **perfectly!**

If you want to know what happened next, WELL...

Cinderella and the Prince whisked themselves off to the palace where they did live HAPPILY EVER AFTER!

(Apart from on Sundays...)

Sundays were the AWFUL day when Gerta and Greta
always chose to visit. But if they ever
got TOO bossy (which they often did)
Cinderella just stuck her fingers
in her ears and blew them a
huge **royal raspberry**...

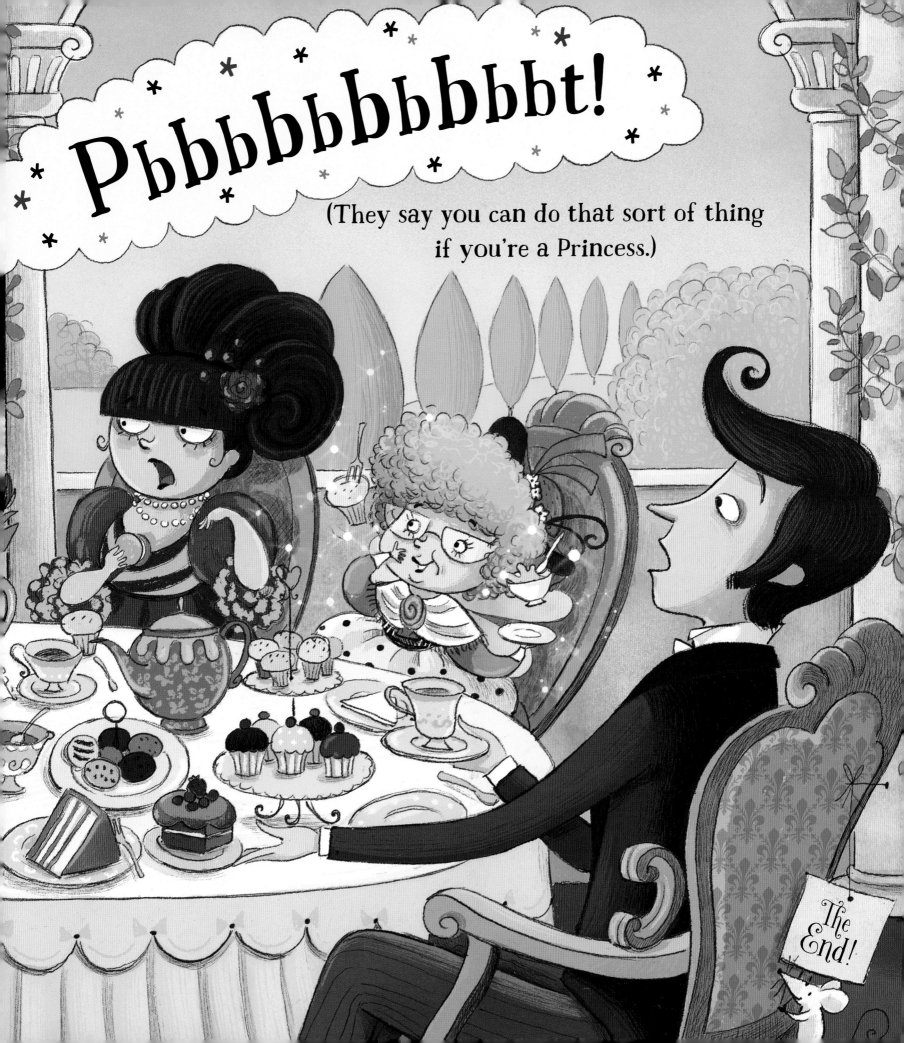